The BIG House

CARAMEL TREE

Harry is sad.
"My house is small," says Harry.

"Can you show me?" asks Joe.

"Come with me," says Harry.

"This is the living room," says Harry.
Joe sits on the big sofa.

"This is the dining room," says Harry.
There is a big table and six big chairs.

11

"The bathroom is down the hallway," says Harry.
There are big plants in the hallway.

13

 Chapter 2 Small Rooms

Harry shows the bedroom.
There is a big bed.

15

Harry shows the attic.
There are many old things.

Harry shows the kitchen.
There is a big fridge.

"What's in the garage?" says Joe.
"It's full," says Harry.

"My house is small," says Harry.
"But your yard is BIG," says Joe.

Harry and Joe move the sofa.

They move the table and the chairs.

They move the bed.

29

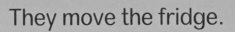

They move the fridge.

"Your furniture is very BIG," says Joe.
"Now your house is BIG!"

33